NES

Dear Parent:
Your child's love of reading starts here!

Every child learns to read in a different way and at his or her own speed. Some go back and forth between reading levels and read favorite books again and again. Others read through each level in order. You can help your young reader improve and become more confident by encouraging his or her own interests and abilities. From books your child reads with you to the first books he or she reads alone, there are I Can Read Books for every stage of reading:

SHARED READING
Basic language, word repetition, and whimsical illustrations, ideal for sharing with your emergent reader

BEGINNING READING
Short sentences, familiar words, and simple concepts for children eager to read on their own

READING WITH HELP
Engaging stories, longer sentences, and language play for developing readers

READING ALONE
Complex plots, challenging vocabulary, and high-interest topics for the independent reader

ADVANCED READING
Short paragraphs, chapters, and exciting themes for the perfect bridge to chapter books

I Can Read Books have introduced children to the joy of reading since 1957. Featuring award-winning authors and illustrators and a fabulous cast of beloved characters, I Can Read Books set the standard for beginning readers.

A lifetime of discovery begins with the magical words "I Can Read!"

Visit www.icanread.com for information on enriching your child's reading experience.

For Huckleberry, who loves
the garden most of all
—A.S.C.

For our wonderful editor,
Anne Hoppe
—P.S.

I Can Read Book® is a trademark of HarperCollins Publishers.

Library of Congress Cataloging-in-Publication Data is available.
ISBN 978-0-06-193505-3 (trade bdg.) — ISBN 978-0-06-193504-6 (pbk.)

12 13 14 15 16   SCP   10 9 8 7 6 5 4 3 2 1   ❖   First Edition

My First
SHARED READING

Biscuit
in the Garden

story by ALYSSA SATIN CAPUCILLI
pictures by PAT SCHORIES

HARPER
An Imprint of HarperCollinsPublishers

Come along, Biscuit.
It is time to visit
the garden.
Woof, woof!

The garden is filled
with so many things, Biscuit.
Woof, woof!

Just look at all the flowers
and plants.
Woof, woof!

You found a butterfly, Biscuit.
Woof, woof!

You found a worm, too.

Woof!

Silly puppy!

Don't dig now!

Woof, woof!

Oh, Biscuit.

You found a little bird.

Is the little bird hungry?

Woof, woof!

Tweet!

Let's feed the bird, Biscuit.

Woof, woof!

Wait, Biscuit.

What do you see?

Woof!

Two more little birds!

Tweet! Tweet!
Here, little birds.

Here is some bird seed.

Woof, woof!

Come along, Biscuit.

There's lots more to see.

Tweet!

Woof, woof!

Tweet! Tweet! Woof!

Oh no, Biscuit.

Not the bird seed!

Woof, woof!

Tweet! Tweet! Tweet! Tweet!
Just look at all
of the birds now!

Woof, woof!
The garden is filled
with so many things, Biscuit.

Woof, woof!
But you filled the garden
with lots of birds, too!
Tweet! Tweet!

Woof!